PEANUT BUTTER & ~~JELLY~~ ALIENS

A ZOMBIE CULINARY TALE

Words by

Joe McGee

Pictures by

Charles Santoso

ABRAMS BOOKS FOR YOUNG READERS • NEW YORK

THE ILLUSTRATIONS IN THIS BOOK WERE MADE DIGITALLY.

Library of Congress Cataloging—in—Publication Data has been
applied for and may be obtained from the Library of Congress.
ISBN: 978—1—4197—2530—2

Text copyright © 2017 Joe McGee
Illustrations copyright © 2017 Charles Santoso
Book design by Chad W. Beckerman

Printed and bound in China
10 9 8 7 6 5 4 3 2 1

ABRAMS The Art of Books
115 West 18th Street, New York, NY 10011
abramsbooks.com

For Jessica,
the most amazing girl in Quirkville.
—J.McG.

For all the Abigail Zinks out there.
—C.S.

Quirkville was a quiet little town. The kind of place where the people and the zombies lived in peace and shared their peanut butter and jelly sandwiches.
All was well in Quirkville . . .

. . . until the aliens landed.

Reginald was the first to see them.

"SPLOINK!?" said an alien.

He seemed awfully interested in Reginald's pizza.

"SPLOINK!?" said the rest of the aliens.

"Pizza?" said Reginald, offering the alien a taste of his slice.

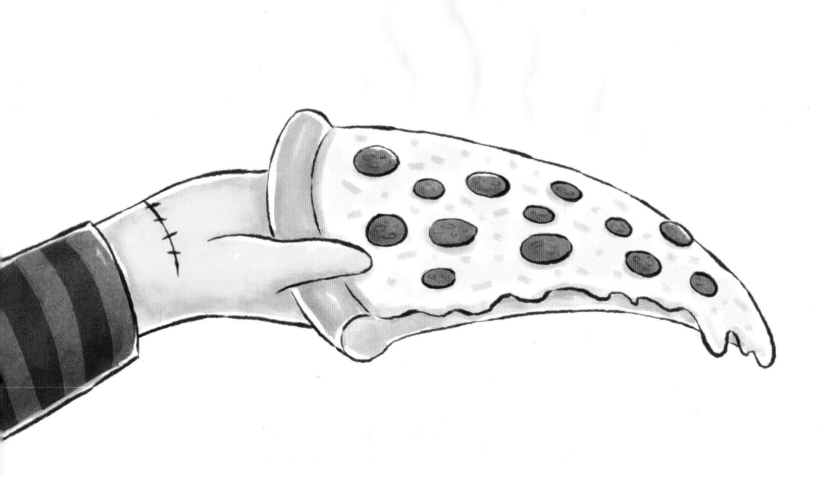

But when the alien bit into the pizza, his antennae quivered and his tentacles shook. He did not look happy.

"SPLOINK!?"
the aliens all bellowed,
shaking their tentacles in the air.

"Well hello there," said Abigail Zink, the smartest girl in Quirkville. "Welcome to Quirkville."

"SPLOINK?" said the aliens.

"I don't know what they want," said Reginald, "but it's not pizza."

Then suddenly,

BRAZZAP-SPLAT!

The aliens zapped the corner café with their blasters,
covering it in cosmic grape jelly.

Greta flipped some grilled cheese
sandwiches onto their plates.

RAZZAP-SPLAT!

The aliens coated her with cosmic grape jelly.

The aliens marched into Oscar's Grocery. "SPLOINK!?" they said.
"Pickles?" said Oscar. "Peanuts? Pistachio ice cream?"

BRAZZAP—SPLAT!

Oscar was covered, too.

"Quirkville is in a sticky situation!" said the mayor.
"I declare a state of emergency!"

"That's it!" said Abigail Zink. "A sticky situation!
What goes best with jelly?"
"Peanut butter!" said Reginald.

"Citizens of Quirkville!" said Abigail Zink. "Gather up all your peanut butter!"

"Fellow zombies!" moaned Reginald. "We need your PB&J sandwiches!"

"SPLOINK!?"

said the aliens, marching towards town hall.

The aliens lifted their blaster-clutching tentacles, ready to squirt cosmic grape jelly all over town hall.

The townspeople froze. The zombies moaned.
The mayor's poodle yipped and yapped.

"One big jar of delicious peanut butter coming right up," said Abigail Zink. She handed the peanut butter to Reginald.

"SPLOINK?" asked Reginald, opening the peanut butter.

"SPLOINK?" said the aliens, dipping their tentacles into the jar.

No sooner had the aliens tasted the peanut butter than their single eyes opened wide and they dropped their blasters. "SPLOINK!" they said.

"MMMM," hummed the aliens, devouring the sweet jelly and sticky peanut butter sandwiches. "SPLOINK!!"

"Well how about that," said the mayor. "They came all this way for PB&J!"
"You mean, SPLOINK!" said Abigail Zink.
The aliens were sorry for the misunderstanding and cleaned up their cosmic grape jelly mess. The people and zombies of Quirkville accepted their apology with warm smiles and hearty handshakes.

Reginald and Abigail Zink, however, had a great idea. They had a better use for the aliens' cosmic grape jelly. Why put it in blasters, when you could put it on a sandwich? Soon, Quirkville had a brand new PB&J restaurant with sandwiches that were out of this world . . .

Complete with interstellar delivery!